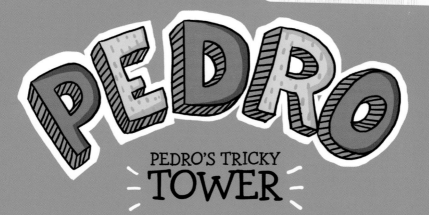

PEDRO'S TRICKY
⋛ TOWER ⋚

by Fran Manushkin

illustrated by
Tammie Lyon

PICTURE WINDOW BOOKS
a capstone imprint

Pedro is published by Picture Window Books,
a Capstone Imprint
1710 Roe Crest Drive
North Mankato, Minnesota 56003
www.mycapstone.com

Text © 2018 Fran Manushkin
Illustrations © 2018 Picture Window Books

Library of Congress Cataloging-in-Publication Data is available
on the Library of Congress website

ISBN: 978-1-5158-1903-5 (library binding)
ISBN: 978-1-5158-1905-9 (paperback)
ISBN: 978-1-5158-1907-3 (eBook PDF)

Summary: Pedro's class is building a tower out of paper cups to see who can build the tallest tower. Pedro loves to build, but he's got a big problem. Troublemaker Roddy is on his team.

Designer: Tracy McCabe
Photo Credit: iStockphoto:huronphoto, pg 29
Design Elements: Shutterstock

Printed and bound in the USA.
112017   010953R

Table of Contents

Chapter 1
A Tricky Project

Pedro loved to build. He

helped his father make a tree

house. He helped his grandpa

build a fireplace.

One day, his teacher,

Miss Winkle, told the class, "I

have a tricky building project

for you."

"Yay!" yelled Roddy. "I love tricks. I play them on people all the time."

"That's not the kind of tricky I mean," said Miss Winkle. "We are going to try to build the tallest tower."

"That's easy!" bragged
Pedro. "All we need are lots
of bricks."

"We are not using bricks,"

said Miss Winkle. "We are

using nineteen paper cups.

You will be working in teams."

Barry and JoJo were on Katie Woo's team. Sophie was on Pedro's team. So was Roddy!

"Watch out!" warned

Katie. "R-O-D-D-Y spells

T-R-O-U-B-L-E."

Chapter 2

Time to Build

Miss Winkle told the teams,

"Before you build, you need

to plan."

"I don't need to plan," said

Pedro. "I know what to do."

Pedro began piling up paper cups. He tried to build high, but the towers kept falling down.

Roddy put four paper cups on his head.

"Watch out!" he joked. "My towers are falling down too."

Pedro and Sophie tried again and again. But the cups kept falling.

"Oh, boy!" said Pedro.

"I wish we had some bricks."

Then it was time for recess.

Roddy told Pedro, "Forget

the tower! Let's see who can

do the most handstands. I

know I'll win!"

Roddy flipped upside down

and back again. Pedro tried it.

He kept falling down.

"Watch me and learn,"

said Roddy.

Pedro did watch Roddy.

Then he began thinking.

"That's it!" Pedro yelled.

"You showed me how to build

the tallest tower."

Chapter 3
The Tallest Tower

After recess, Pedro ran back
to class. He said, "Let's put
some of the cups right side up
and some upside down."

Pedro and Sophie began
to build.

"Let me help," said Roddy.

He began piling up the cups.

Their tower got higher and higher. It did not fall! It was the tallest tower!

"Way to go!" said Miss Winkle.

Roddy couldn't stop smiling. He told Pedro, "I knew we could do it!"

He gave Pedro a high five.

After school, Pedro said, "Want to help me fix my tree house?"

"Cool!" said Roddy. "I'll race you there."

They both won.

About the Author

Fran Manushkin is the author
of many popular picture books,
including *Happy in Our Skin*; *Baby,
Come Out!*; *Latkes and Applesauce:
A Hanukkah Story*; *The Tushy
Book*; *Big Girl Panties*; and *Big
Boy Underpants*. Fran writes on
her beloved Mac computer in New York City,
without the help of her two naughty cats,
Chaim and Goldy.

About the Illustrator

Tammie Lyon began her love for
drawing at a young age while
sitting at the kitchen table with
her dad. She continued her love
of art and eventually attended
the Columbus College of Art
and Design, where she earned
a bachelor's degree in fine art. After a brief
career as a professional ballet dancer, she decided
to devote herself full-time to illustration. Today she
lives with her husband, Lee, in Cincinnati, Ohio.
Her dogs, Gus and Dudley, keep her company as she
works in her studio.

Glossary

bragged (BRAGD)—talked about how good you are at something

recess (REE-sess)—a break from schoolwork, often outside

tower (TOU-ur)—a tall structure that is thin in relation to its height

tricky (TRIK-ee)—difficult in an unexpeceted way, requiring careful thought or handling

warned (WORND)—told a person about a bad or dangerous thing that could happen

Let's Talk

1. Pedro likes to build things. How was his tower building project different from other things he had built?

2. Pedro didn't make a plan, even though his teacher said they should. How might the story have been different if his team had made a plan?

3. Do you think that Pedro and Roddy will be friends now? Why or why not?

Let's Write

1. What would you like to build? What supplies would you need? Write a paragraph about it.

2. List five adjectives (describing words) that describe Pedro's team's tower. Then choose one word and write a sentence with it.

3. The students worked in teams. It is important to be a good team member when you are working as a group. Write three rules for being a good team member.

Stack Cups for Sport!

In this story, Pedro, JoJo, and Roddy have to build a tall tower out of paper cups. It was hard, but they did it and won the contest.

But guess what? Stacking and moving cups quickly is an actual sport! It's called Sport Stacking, and competitions are held all over the country. Kids are given plastic cups. They must follow strict rules to stack them and move them up and down and back and forth as quickly as possible.

Doing this is tricky! It takes concentration, quickness, and focus. You can't daydream when you are moving cups around at record speed! Sometimes kids work in pairs, which is even trickier!

To find out more about Sport Stacking, watch videos of champs, and find Sports Stacking tournaments, visit www.thewssa.com

What kind of nails do carpenters hate to hammer?
fingernails

Why did the carpenter quit making wooden cars?
They wooden go.

Knock, knock
Who's there?
Hammer
Hammer who?
Would you like hammer bacon with those eggs?

WITH PEDRO!

🔨 Why did the carpenter fall asleep on the job?
He was board.

🔨 What is the tallest tower in town?
the library — it has lots of stories

🔨 What animal can jump higher than Pedro's tower?
any animal — the tower can't jump

THE FUN DOESN'T STOP HERE!

Discover more at www.capstonekids.com

- Videos & Contests
- Games & Puzzles
- Friends & Favorites
- Authors & Illustrators

Find cool websites and more books like this one at www.facthound.com. Just type in the Book ID: 9781515819035 and you're ready to go!